A MODEL FOR MURDER

A NOVELLA

BY
SIR PATRICK BIJOU

Prologue

Follow the Compelling Story of Candace Kane and Get Ready to Have Your Mind Blown With Twists of This Murder Mystery Thriller.

My name is Candace Kane, and I have extraordinary power – I'm an Empath. This power is unlike any other, and I don't really know how to explain it to you in a way so you can understand.

I have these visions. I see the events and feel the emotions that aren't mine. I hate these damned visions. Well, I hate them sometimes, most often when I feel another person's pain and sorrow. But usually, I only see other people's joys, quarrels, and everything in between. Those are bearable.

It was a long time ago when I found about this power. I discovered that strong emotions have the tendency to latch themselves onto something that person was holding or touching. That's why I'm not particularly eager to touch strange things.

But this time, I didn't mean to. It was an accident. He was there in the water...floating. I tried to pull him out, and I touched his necklace. Instead of showing me his joy, that cursed necklace showed me the man's final moments – his last breath while he was brutally murdered.

Sherrif thinks that it was an accident, but I saw it clearly as a day – he was murdered. Now I need to find a way to convince Sherrif without revealing myself. How on earth can I do that?!

Enjoy the thrill, suspense, and the skillfully crafted twists, and find out if Candace will be able to reveal who the mysterious murderer was!

TABLE OF CONTENTS

CHAPTER ONE

The rising sun gently caressed the mountains west of Lake Tahoe with bright fingers. It revealed their stony grandeur in a blaze of glory that hardly relieved the gloom on the beach as I ran. The temperature was just starting to nudge up from the upper thirties. That was Lake Tahoe summers for you. You got enjoyable warm days and bitingly cold nights.

I was so busy enjoying the view that I almost missed the man floating face up in the shallows. I skidded to a halt in surprise, my braided red hair swinging wildly at the sudden change in momentum.

My breath fogged the air around me as I stared in shock, but his breath didn't. The water was cold enough to kill and he was just floating in it.

I looked around franticly for help. The tall pine trees to my right shielded the still sleeping town of Angel's Point from my sight. It was almost as if I was alone in the wilderness. I had my doubts about a little slip of a woman like myself being able to pull a full-grown man out of the water, but given when and where I was, I didn't have much of a choice.

The water felt ice cold as I ran to the man's side. My running sweats were instantly soaked. In the growing light, I could see his wide eyes staring off into infinity. I could also see that he wasn't breathing.

I grabbed his black windbreaker at the neck and pulled him toward the shore with all my might. He moved a few inches, his body scraping along the shallow bottom. I grabbed the front of his jacket and pulled again.

That brought me into water only a few inches deep. One more heave and I'd have his head and shoulders on the beach. I renewed my grip on his collar and pulled. Something coldly metallic kissed my left hand and I fell heavily on my butt at the rim of the beach. I had a moment to blink at the small medallion on a chain around his neck before I was plunged into darkness.

It took a moment to recognize what I was seeing. It was a vision and I had no choice but to ride it out to the end. There was no breaking the hold of the curse.

I was standing on a dock looking out over Lake Tahoe at night. Well, technically the man was standing there but the only thoughts in my head were mine. I might have to ride his emotions, but his thoughts were absent. Thank God.

An overhead light shed an eerie glow, but didn't fully dispel the disquieting darkness around me. There was a cabin cruiser moored to my right. I could barely make out part of the boat's name emblazoned on the white hull - "something Valkyrie."

The view over the lake was a familiar one for me. I saw almost this exact view from my bedroom window at the Lodge. But this wasn't the Lodge's dock. That left only the dock at Angel's Point Inn on the other end of the mile-long stretch of beach from the Lodge.

I wanted to look around – no, I wanted to turn around and run. Alas, neither of those things was going to happen. At this point, the man was providing all my sensory input. I could only see what the man had seen, and I could only sense what he felt at that moment. The overwhelming emotion that I tasted was his anger. If I was lucky, I might get a clue as to why he had been so angry.

I couldn't just keep thinking of him as "the man." That never felt right when I had a vision. John Doe was better. True, too.

Behind me, I heard a creak of wood. It might be the sound a boat rubbing against the dock. I knew it wasn't, but I could always hope.

I strained to hear anything more, but only normal sounds from the lake greeted me. That didn't fool me. I knew someone had quietly walked up behind me and was standing there in silence.

John didn't bother turning around. His voice was well articulated and colored by irritation. "I told you I'm not going to stop, so you might as well..."

The sudden kick behind John's left knee was a surprise to both of us. He fell heavily and his wrist flared with pain as he landed heavily on it. Before he could struggle, strong fingers grabbed his hair and slammed his head into something hard.

Pain exploded like a supernova across my consciousness. I knew it wasn't mine, but that didn't lessen the impact one bit. Everything began swirling darkly around me.

John's neck began to burn with pain, but his body went strangely numb. No, not numb... absent. He couldn't seem to breathe. Panic exploded inside his mind. Mine, too.

John's attacker grabbed the collar of his jacket and dragged him to the edge of the pier. There was a brief sensation of falling and then cold, dark water blotted out John's vision. No matter how hard he tried, his arms and legs wouldn't move and he sank into the frigid water.

I felt cold sand against my cheek – my cheek, not his. I opened my eyes. I'd fallen onto my side above John. The vision had ended.

Passing out wasn't a normal side effect of a vision – not that anything about this could be considered normal – but they weren't usually this powerful either. I took a deep breath and tried to sit up, but my body refused to cooperate.

The damned visions just wouldn't leave me alone. They made me different from everyone else and I hated that. I saw things and felt emotions that weren't mine. They were strong and sometimes more painful than I could stand.

I should've known better than to touch a stranger's things. I knew I had to be careful. Strong emotion could imprint itself onto something a person was holding or touching. Metal like that worked all too damned well as a storage device, no matter how long ago the event.

Normally, I only saw other people's quarrels, joys, and everything in between. This time I'd seen murder and I couldn't seem to think.

Strong hands interrupted my fuzzy thoughts as they grabbed my shoulder and rolled me onto my back. I screamed. At least my voice worked.

A man's face loomed over me, dark, curly hair clinging close to his scalp. Opaque obsidian eyes burned with worry.

It's okay," he said. "I won't hurt you."

He wore a dark leather jacket, a plain black T-shirt, and jeans. His shoulders were wide, and his waist was trim. The tight shirt highlighted his well-defined abdominal muscles. I shouldn't have looked but they were right there sitting in plain sight.

It took a moment before I recognized him. His name was Tyrone Walker. We'd gone to high school together. My mother warned me about boys like him. I pressed her for more details eagerly. She told me firmly to steer clear of him. She told me he was dangerous and after watching him from afar, I decided she was right.

He'd been a dark and mysterious figure that rode a motorcycle and had girls dancing around him. They swarmed like moths drawn to a flame. The whispered gossip my friends had passed around about him had both excited and terrified me.

I'd longed to ask him out and see for myself, but I chickened out. However, he did feature prominently in a number of quiet, late-night fantasies. After graduation, he joined the Navy and disappeared from Angel's Point.

"Tyrone Walker?" I asked. "What are you doing here?" Well, that certainly made me sound like an idiot. The damned vision had really taken it out of me.

He blinked in surprise.

"Call me Ty," he said automatically. "Are you okay?"

I struggled to think of a safe, plausible explanation for collapsing and only came up with one that didn't make me sound like a kook. I'd have to go with the weak, girly excuse, as much as I hated people thinking of me like that. This sucked.

"I... I must've fainted." I struggled to a sitting position and stared at the body. "I've never..."

The explanation, as much as it torqued me, satisfied his worry for me. He slipped his jacket around my shoulders, making me suddenly aware I was shivering, and helped me stagger up the beach. I sat heavily in the dry sand and pulled the warm jacket tightly around me. Ty returned to John and started checking him.

"You're Candice Kane, right?" Ty asked. He sounded like he wasn't convinced he remembered the right name. I couldn't blame him. Candy Kane sounded like a gag. One becomes resigned to the jokes and teasing after a while. Mom swears Dad slipped it past her while she was still recovering after giving birth to me. Knowing my dad, it's probably true.

Frankly, I was astounded he remembered my name. "I like Candy better. You remember me?"

The corner of his mouth quirked up as those dark eyes glanced up at me. "How many five foot tall redheads could there be in Angel's Point? Believe me, no one that's seen you once would forget."

He felt John's neck and shook his head. The dawn had finally reached the beach and I took a good look at John. He was dressed in soaked jeans, a dark blue sweater, and a black windbreaker. One foot had a brown loafer but the other was bare. It was difficult to judge his age but he couldn't have been over forty.

"No joy. I'd say he's been in the water for at least several hours, if not all night," Ty said, looking up at me again. "His name is Steven Armstrong. Something hit him hard on the side of his skull. I'd say his neck is broken."

My mouth dropped open. He'd more or less described my vision and he knew the guy's name, too.

"How do you know all that?" I demanded when I could finally speak.

"Let's just say that he's not the first dead body I've seen pulled out of the water." He stood and brushed sand off his pants.

I didn't know how to respond to that. I forced myself to focus. "We need to call the Sheriff's Department." "I called them on my cell when I saw what you were pulling out of the lake." The corner of his mouth quirked up again. "I expect they won't be too pleased with me hanging up on them."

"They do tend to get worked up about things like that," I agreed. I rubbed the bridge of my nose tiredly. "I didn't see you. Where were you hiding?"

He pointed at the trees between the beach and the highway. "I came out here before dawn and was sitting in the trees watching the sun hit the mountains. I saw you coming but I'm ashamed to say I missed the dead body in the dark water. That was incredibly careless of me. I shouldn't have left you with the burden of finding something like this."

It took a moment but I finally decided he was being serious. Men. Who could understand them? We couldn't change the past. Life only went forward.

How did you know his name?" I asked, nodding toward Armstrong.

Ty considered the man expressionlessly. "I work for him. That should be past tense, I suppose."

"Doing what?"

Ty shrugged. "He hired me to help raise a ship from the south end of the lake. The S.S. Tahoe, a ship that used to make the circuit of the lake before there were roads. Her owners intentionally sunk her back in 1940. Armstrong wanted to get her afloat, restore her, and turn her into a floating museum."

I nodded. "The local paper said something about divers going down to it. I seem to remember that it was so deep they couldn't stay more than a few minutes and it was dangerous as hell. How can you recover something like that?"

"Armstrong bought a special deep diving suit from Canada. That's where I come in. I trained in something similar in the Navy. I'm supposed to go down and secure the lifts to the hull and they'll fill them with air and lift the ship."

If Ty thought having a normal conversation next to a dead man was odd, he didn't mention it. With the memory of his death still coloring my emotions, I gratefully seized upon this segue into normality.

We didn't have time to say anything else before I heard a siren wailing in the distance. Ty stood up, brushed the sand from his knees, and took a couple of steps toward the tree-shrouded highway. I slowly followed.

A sheriff's Deputy, Andy Milbank, came trotting out of the trees and took the scene in quickly. He ran to the body and made the same assessment that Ty and I had already made. Like ours, his didn't take more than a few seconds. He stood up and murmured into the microphone clipped to the shoulder of his uniform. It didn't matter that it was too soft for me to make out the words. It was probably in police-speak anyway.

I'd known Andy since we were kids. A year younger than me, he'd made the ritual passes at me during high school, and had taken my polite no with good grace. In a town of four thousand, I ran into him frequently, but never during something like this.

He had his cop face on, all professional and dispassionate. "This is a part of the job I could live without," he said. He nodded at me. "Candy." He raised an eyebrow at Ty. "You look familiar but I can't place the face."

"Tyrone Walker." Ty offered his hand.

A look of recognition dawned in Andy's eyes. "Angel Point's own James Dean. Welcome home, prodigal son." Andy shook Ty's hand. Then he gestured to John, or rather Steven Armstrong.

"Dispatch said a man called this in. Was that you?" Ty nodded. "Dispatch is plenty peeved with you for hanging up on them. What happened here?"

Ty went first. I was grateful to have to time to order my thoughts. Andy jotted our statements down in his notebook in just a few minutes.

I wished I could have given him something more solid than my public story. Even if I could've mentioned the vision, it didn't provide any details about the identity of the killer - other than the fact the victim seemed to know his killer. A fact I was sure the Sheriff's Department would quickly ferret out.

The only nudge I could give him was where I thought Armstrong went into the lake. The sluggish current along the beach did run from the north, as the body and my vision proved. Andy didn't look convinced, but he did pass my hunch on through the radio. There was probably little evidence anyway, so I hoped they would get someone to the dock before a boater messed up the crime scene.

By the time we finished going through our stories another Sheriff's Deputy and a couple of guys in a Coroner's van had pulled up behind Andy's car. The other Deputy brought me a blanket. I tried to return Ty's jacket but he waved my gesture away.

I was starting to wonder what I should do now when Andy returned from his patrol car.

"Senior Deputy Cooper's at the dock," He said. "He'd like you to join him." I knew Cooper well enough. I'd known him since he'd first come to Angel's Point twenty years ago. As the top man around here, he'd be in charge during the investigation. I wasn't sure if that was good news because I thought he was a little unimaginative.

I shrugged and nodded. I needed to see my part of this through. Ty joined me in the back of the patrol car. As I buckled in, I gave him a look. I'd never been in the back of a police car before, but I bet he'd had more than a few trips in one. That would just fit his reputation.

Ty smiled briefly at me. "This is nice. It's so new it doesn't smell like drunken tourists. That's real classy."

"Do you have much experience with cop cars and drunken tourists?" I asked, amused.

"Well, I have been a tourist, and I do have a lot of experience with the back seats of cars. Some were police cars." He waggled his eyebrows at me. "Some weren't." When I just grinned and shook my head, he asked, "In any case, does that count?"

I considered making a smart reply, but opted for ladylike silence instead. From his expression, I gathered I wasn't too successful but he let it pass for the half-mile drive to the Inn.

The Fletchers built the Angel's Point Inn some thirty years ago. When my ex, Calvin Bender, and his new wife Dora had taken over management from her parents three years ago, they carried the modern concept to what I saw as a distasteful extreme. Their remodeling was all glass, chrome, brass, and sharp angles. It looked so modern now that I couldn't stand it. It was very out of place here in rustic Angel's Point. Anyone who found this monstrosity pretty had all their taste in their mouth.

Yet, somehow, the redesign of the Inn had gotten all the requisite approvals and in the Lake Tahoe basin that was supposed to be difficult. I darkly suspected bribery every chance I could.

My mother said I was just letting my distaste for Calvin and Dora color my opinions. I disagreed, though I had plenty of reason to dislike Calvin and Dora.

Our marriage had been a short one. I caught Calvin on our couch with Dora less than a month after our honeymoon. Those who said our divorce was acrimonious were guilty of gross understatement. The Israeli-Palestinian conflict was less divisive. Frankly, if it weren't for the total support of my family and the fact I loved Kane Lodge, I probably would've left Angel's Point.

Marrying Calvin had been a mistake. Everyone warned me what a slug he was but I refused to listen. Dora, on the other hand, I knew would do anything to hurt me. She'd made school a living hell when we were growing up. This wasn't something she picked up from her parents, either. Her mom and dad were nice people, and kept the competition between our families from becoming personal. We'd even had dinner every couple of months until they retired to Hawaii.

Dora settled on a scorched earth policy for dealing with me in middle school and thereafter. I suppose seducing my brand new husband and wooing the two-timing bastard during the divorce was the ultimate in slap-in-the-face rivalry by the overly made up skank.

I took a deep breath and forced those thoughts from my mind. Calvin and Dora would have to take their turn. I tried to open the door when the car pulled to a stop, but the handle didn't work. Duh! It was a police car.

Andy let us out and escorted us around the outside of the Inn. That was good. With any luck, I'd be gone before Calvin or Dora cornered me. I wanted to see them less than the dead body.

Deputy Cooper stood about halfway down the dock looking out over the water with his hands in his pockets. He wasn't much to look at, with an unfortunate comb-over and a belly like a walrus. He waved for us to join him.

"Morning, Deputy Cooper," I said when we drew close.

He took off his uniform cap and used his handkerchief to wipe his forehead. Even in the cool temperatures, he was sweating. "Miss Kane, I'm sorry you had to find such a terrible thing." "Unlike Mister Armstrong, I'll get over it," I said. I heard Ty chuckle at my dark humor.

"You were right," Cooper said. "I'm pretty sure he went into the water right here."

Crime scene tape sealed off several of the knee-high pilings and something dark stained the wood on one. I swallowed heavily.

"Is that blood?" I asked, my stomach feeling queasy.

"Looks to be," Cooper agreed with a nod. "We'll get some samples and send them off to the County seat. It looks like he hit pretty hard. I figure it stunned him and he fell into the water and drowned."

I nodded. The fact that Armstrong had a broken neck would come out sooner or later. The challenge was going to be figuring out how to steer Cooper toward the fact that it wasn't an accident.

"But that's not all," he continued. "Look at this." He pointed at a smeared streak on the planks near the stained piling. "Grease. It suggests how things might have happened."

"Um..." I said delicately. "Isn't it too soon to be saying that? You need to look at everything first, don't you? Like on _CSI: New York_?"

"New York?" Ty asked. "Why not Miami?"

I'd forgotten he was standing behind me. "Because I can't stand that red-haired guy. I think my ex-husband has more personality."

Cooper nodded. "We'll look at every bit of evidence. I found a shoe on the dock that sounds like a match for the one still on Mister Armstrong. There's some grease on its sole. Like I said, it's not certain but it is one possibility."

I didn't like the direction this seemed to be going. It might look like an accidental death to everyone but me but they _had_ to look into it as a murder.

I was considering the best way to move the conversation that way when a voice I detested called from behind me. My skin crawled. It was like knowing Darth Vader was standing right behind you.

"Deputy Cooper." Calvin's voice was smooth, like pond scum.

I forced my expression into a pleasant fa+ade and turned to face him. I was less than overjoyed to see he had Dora with him. Whoever said 'no good deed goes unpunished' was dead on the money. I winced mentally at my poor choice of words.

Some might describe Calvin as a distinguished looking man in his mid-thirties, typically dressed in slacks and a yuppie sweater. His brown hair was prematurely graying at the temples and he looked like a perfect gentleman.

I usually described him in less exalted terms.

In a fashion blunder of the first order, Dora was dressed in an outfit matching her slime husband, my ex, Calvin. Sad to say, she looked better over-dressed in her usual designer trash. She overshadowed me by six inches and one look at her chest would convince anyone she was a proponent of body enhancements. I plastered a fake smile on my face for Cooper's benefit.

Calvin pointedly ignored me. No doubt determined to raise my blood pressure. Dora shot mental death rays in my direction.

"What brings you out so early?" he asked. "Is something wrong?"

"I'm afraid so," Cooper said with a nod to Dora. "Ma'am. Does the name Steven Armstrong mean anything to you?"

Calvin and Dora exchanged glances. "He's a guest," Calvin admitted. "Why?"

"Well," Cooper said slowly, "I'm afraid there's been an accident."

"We don't know that," I said.

"What are you blathering about?" Dora asked, her eyes narrowing at me before skewering Cooper. "What's going on here?" "I'm afraid that Mister Armstrong is dead," Cooper said. "There's some indication he went in the water here."

Dora's eyes widened and she rounded on me. "And you're trying to spin this as something other than a terrible accident? You spiteful bitch!"

She started for me; her fingers extended like claws. Calvin yanked her up short like a dog that had reached the end of his chain when by grabbing her jacket. She snarled at him wordlessly but subsided.

Calvin stared at me with lordly indifference. "Candy never got over me leaving her, you know. It's made her bitter." He turned back to Cooper. "This is terrible news. I'm horrified. We'll cooperate in any way you need."

I stared at him, astounded beyond words. That was the most _outrageous_ thing I'd ever heard. The getting over business, anyway. Leave it to the self-centered jerk to turn someone's death into a chance to take a shot at me.

It was par for the course, though. We made the Hatfield's and McCoy's seem like a girl fight after school. This, however, was going too far.

Ty stepped between us before I got over my shocked outrage and throttled either one of them. "Everyone take a deep breath," he said calmly. "No one's saying there was foul play.

Candy's just saying nobody should rush to judgment."

Calvin dismissed Ty with a look. "You don't know her like we do, Mister Walker. She'll do anything to get even with us. She's a small woman in every respect. Take my advice and steer clear of her. In any case, this is none of your business so stay out of it."

Ty smiled benignly but I could see a gleam in his eyes. If Calvin had gone to school with Ty, he'd have known he'd just made a serious mistake. Too bad for him.

Calvin spared me another glance. "Why are you here again, Candy? Don't you have something else to do? Someone else to bother?"

Deputy Cooper shook his head tiredly. "Don't get your shorts in a twist. I brought her here as part of my investigation. She stays till I'm done with her."

I'd said my piece so it was time to let it go. "I've told you what I know. If you have any other questions give me a call."

Cooper nodded and slipped his hat back on. "Thanks for your help, Miss Kane."

I nodded as graciously as I could and let Ty steer me around my ex and his skank while considered and rejected making another lunge for her. That superior smirk on his face just made me want to scream.

We were almost past when Ty's right foot abruptly slipped sideways and he staggered heavily to the left. I grabbed him but all that did was get me dragged along with him as he started to go down.

He would have fallen, except his shoulder rammed into Dora's and sent her crashing into Calvin. Calvin shot off the side of the dock and into the water with a tremendous splash before he even knew what was happening. Dora teetered on the brink for a moment, her arms wind milling frantically for balance, before she followed her husband into the cold water with a scream.

Ty stood there with an artful expression of consternation on his face. "Oh, dear." He shrugged to the deputy. "I must've slipped on something." He looked over at the drenched couple. "Sorry about that. You really need to clean up this dock. So many slipping incidents might cause a lawsuit."

I stood there in awe of him as Cooper began trying to fish them out while they screamed at us. "Let's go to the Lodge and get some breakfast. I'd like to catch up."

"Good call. You need a lift home and you'll love my car."

The morning was looking up after all.

I laughed when I finally saw Ty's car. It was hard to miss. It stood out like a stripper leading a church service.

It was a sleek black muscle car with a supercharger rising like a chrome fist from the center of the hood. I didn't know who manufactured the original chassis, but it was obvious extensive work had gone into it since then. It looked fast, powerful, and utterly impractical for a sub-alpine area like the Tahoe basin. It virtually sat up and begged to scream down some long, straight desert highway.

I put my hands on my hips and looked up at Ty. "I can't believe you bought Mad Max's car." As far as I could tell it was a perfect reproduction of the car Mel Gibson had driven in the movie Mad Max.

He ran his hand across the hood and grinned. "I didn't buy her; I built her. You like?"

"You know this is a pretty impractical car for around here, right? You'll rip the bottom off if you go off-road, or drive into the lake if you floor it. The gas mileage probably sucks, too." Even as I ticked off the reasons it was impractical, I couldn't help but run my hands along its beautiful lines. I laughed guiltily when I caught myself wondering how fast it could go.

He smiled smugly at me, patiently waiting for a positive reaction from me.

"Okay!" I relented. "It's impractical, but it's hot."

Only then did he hold the passenger door open for me. The seat was made of dark leather and felt buttery soft. I wished my couch felt this nice.

He tossed his jacket into the back seat and climbed in beside me. As he buckled in, I stared at his arms and chest with something approaching awe. Shave his head and he'd look like Vin Diesel, only hunkier. The tight tee shirt showed his wide chest and flat abdomen off nicely.

Ty cleared his throat.

I yanked my eyes up to his face guiltily and caught him grinning at me. I looked away and fumbled with the seatbelt to cover the sudden flush I felt creeping up my neck. The pregnant silence grew as I looked at the seatbelt in confusion. There were a lot more than two belts to clip together.

"Let me help you with that," he said in an amused tone. "I put in five - point restraints and a steel roll bar, just in case." He gathered up the straps in his large hands and slid them together just below my bellybutton. His hands were rough and had a couple of old scars. They looked strong. They also felt warmer than they had any right to be.

That sparked a rush of heat in my gut that made me blush an even deeper red. His hands didn't linger, but his satisfied smile told me my poker face needed some work.

The car started with a grumbling roar. Even idling it sounded as powerful as a locomotive. He let it warm up and turned on the heater as soon as the engine was hot enough.

"Ready?" he asked as he dropped it into gear. He stomped the gas and pulled out so fast the tires squealed.

Kane Lodge was a sprawling stone and rough timber building that dominated the tip of Angel's Point Peninsula. Its two stories height might not seem like much until you took into account how much it sprawled.

My grandfather and great-grandfather built Kane Lodge eighty years ago, and it was still going strong with the fourth generation now in control.

I left Ty in the lobby and raced back to my suite and showered in record time. I slid into a nice pair of slacks and a loose white blouse before brushing my hair out and tying into a ponytail. I allowed myself a slinky light blue bra. He'd never see it but I'd know it was there.

My orange cat, Screamer, was standing on the stand beside the door waiting for me as I started out. She wanted attention and she wanted it now. My purse, however, was not on the stand. I must've left it at mom's last night.

I picked Screamer up and held her in my arms like a baby, scratching her chin. She tolerated it for a few seconds before starting to squirm and voice her protest. I didn't try to stop her when she did what she'd wanted to do in the first place and climbed onto my shoulder. She stood there for half-a-minute like a furry parrot with green eyes before hopping down and sauntering to the kitchen, her tail curved into a question mark.

"Later, Fur Baby," I consoled her. "I'll feed you this evening." Every cat acted like they were one meal away from starving to death.

I grabbed the master key from the coat hook beside my front door and walked further down the private hallway to Mom's door. All the family had rooms in a little dogleg at the back of the building. My mother's was at the end of the hall here on the second floor. Her room was between mine and my absent brother's. Frank decided he wanted to be a movie special effects man after seeing a TV special on it when he was seven. Determined was hardly adequate to describe how devoted he was to learning everything he could about his obsession. Mom and Dad supported him without restrictions. At least until the incident. Then Mom forbade the use of accelerants inside the Lodge.

I figured Mom was probably still asleep so I opened the door quietly and let myself in without a knock. I'd just grab my purse and scoot back out.

I made it into the middle of her living room before I heard a soft noise that sounded like it was coming from her bedroom. It was so soft I couldn't identify it. I suppose she might've left the TV on after she went to bed. I weighed my odds and decided to keep going.

A small lamp cast a dim glow from beside the dark leather couch. It put out just enough light for me to avoid tripping over the walnut coffee table. I spotted my purse sitting on the couch. Mission accomplished!

I'd just grabbed it when I heard another sound from Mom's room. It was still soft, but this time I was able to make it out. It sounded like a groan.

My heart turned to ice. Had she fallen and hurt herself? Three quick steps brought me to her bedroom door. I grabbed the knob and was in the process of rushing into her room when she groaned again and I realized that wasn't the sound of pain. I froze, my eyes huge.

The murmur of what sounded like a male voice and the gentle creak of her bed echoed softly through the door. She had someone in there with her. Holy crap!

I slapped my hand across my mouth and repressed the loud "Eeeeeewwwwww" that struggled to escape. I did not want to even think about my mother having sex!

I backed away from the door with legs that felt like jelly. I needed to get out of here quickly before I found out intimate details of her love life I'd rather not know.

Retreating quickly in a dark room that wasn't mine turned out to be mistake. I backed into the recliner and flopped over the arm with a barely repressed squeak. The chair reclined and the footrest popped out with a clank.

I froze. Maybe they were too busy to hear me. Please, God, don't let them come out! At least don't let them come out naked. My heart thundered in my ears.

"Did you hear something?" I faintly heard my mother ask. The reply – definitely male –

was too indistinct to identify. They were coming out!

I pulled the seat back into its upright position. The sound of the metal springs in the chair sounded as loud as a brass band marching back and forth in Mom's living room to my panicked ears. I half sprinted and half tiptoed for the front door.

Mom's bed creaked loudly as someone climbed out of it. Heavy steps told me someone was heading toward her door.

I snatched Mom's front door open and whirled through it, stopping the door from slamming at the last second. I eased it closed with a soft click just as I heard her bedroom door open.

I hurled myself down the short access hallway that served the family quarters like a frightened gazelle. I didn't stop until I went through the locked door separating the family wing from the rest of the lodge. Only then did I allow myself to brace my heaving shoulders against the wall and catch my breath.

My mom had a man back in her life. The thought made my head spin. She hadn't dated once since dad died four years ago. I mentally amended that thought: she hadn't that I'd ever known about. And now she was sleeping with someone. At least it sure looked like someone spent the night with her. I wondered how long I had been oblivious.

This was going to take some getting used to, even though I'd been pushing her to start dating. Hell, I'd almost bullied her at times over the last year to find a gentleman friend even if she didn't want a long-term relationship. She'd become a recluse and I'd become worried she wasn't ever going to come out of her shell.

Part of me wondered if she'd been playing a game all this time, but I dismissed that as just not being in my mother's character. I laughed a bit at my foolishness. I'd pushed her to find someone, and now I was suspicious the moment she had. I was being silly. This was great news. Still, I wondered and worried about the new man in her life.

I took a deep breath and settled my shoulders. I needed to deal with one thing at a time. There would be time enough to dig the filtered details out of mom later. For now, I had more pressing problems.

Ty had settled in one of the comfortable leather chairs scattered across the hardwood floor of the lobby by the time I came down the staircase.

It was a huge, wide-open space of open-framed timber and deep carpet. An array of stuffed animals lined the walls, giving the place a rustic appeal.

He was right in front of an absolutely monstrous fireplace sunk low in one of the deep leather seats. Dad used to tell me that they roasted boar in it when he was a boy and I could believe it.

Ty rose smoothly to his feet. "You look great."

I shook my head at his smooth comment and smiled. "Thank you. Come on, let's get something to eat."

He smiled and followed me into the restaurant. Grandfather had built it with the same theme as the rest of the Lodge: open timber rafters, polished wood floors, and quarried stone walls. Pictures of the lodge and my ancestors hung everywhere inside it, providing a glimpse of Angel's Point as it had been years ago.

The family booth at the back of the restaurant had a picture of my parents, Frank, and me. We'd been fishing on the lakeshore and were showing off our catches. My Dad was grinning like there was no tomorrow and holding my Mom tightly. Every time I saw this picture, I missed him again.

Ty looked at me and then at me in the picture after we took our seats. I'd been coltish back then. I must've been thirteen or fourteen, though I looked younger. I remember Dad telling me I was growing like a weed and eating like a swarm of locusts. The irony of me barely reaching five feet and balancing the scales at a hundred pounds was still darkly funny.

I flagged down the lead waitress and we ordered breakfast and coffee. I kept my order to an English muffin and jelly. Ty ordered the biggest platter on the menu. When she had it all, I added one more thing.

"Do me a favor, Karen," I said. "Keep the seating to the front for as long as you can. We'd like a little privacy."

Karen's eyes widened for just a moment, and then she smiled knowingly and nodded before sauntering back to get our food started.

I shook my head ruefully. I knew damned well what that look and that smile of Karen's meant. In less than ten minutes, everyone who worked at the Lodge would know I was here with Ty. It was bad enough that everyone who spread Karen's gossip would assume I was dating the good looking guy. Worse, based on Karen's reaction, they would be surprised. It wasn't like I was living in a nunnery or something. I'd just been busy for the last... Year? Had it really been a year? God, I'd been acting almost as badly as mom!

I shook my head and watched Ty watching me. He was intent, with a hint of amusement in his dark eyes.

"You've changed since high school," Ty said. "You were shy back then. I almost asked you out."

My heart seemed to stop for a moment before it started thumping twice as fast as before. I settled my face in a disbelieving frown. "Me? Whatever in the world for? There were plenty of prettier girls, more popular girls."

Maybe more popular, but not prettier. Don't sell yourself short."

I laughed at his pun, intentional or not. "But I am short. Thank you, though. I wish I'd known that back then. Speaking of high school, where did you disappear to and what've you been up to?"

His dark eyes twinkled. "I'd rather talk about you. That's a much more interesting subject. Tell me about Candy."

I was flattered at his attention and I felt my smile widen. "Flatterer. Well, there's not a lot to tell. I went to UCLA and got a degree in hotel management to help Mom and Dad at the Lodge. Since Dad passed on I've been managing directly."

"I'm sorry to hear about your dad. The few times I saw him around town he seemed like a nice guy. Is your mom holding up okay?"

I shrugged. "She's doing all right, I suppose. It's been four years since his heart attack and I've seen signs she's seeing people again. I've got my fingers crossed." "I'm glad to hear that. As I recall, she shouldn't have any problem finding interested men."

My eyebrow quirked. "And how do you know that?"

He grinned. "Back when we were in high school, your mom made quite an impression when she came by the school to pick you up. I recall quite a few guys who would've jumped if she snapped her fingers."

I laughed loud enough to get looks from the other diners. "As I recall," I said when I finally stopped laughing, "the bar is kinda low for high school boys. If the woman in question has most of the required body parts and doesn't have a beard bigger than Ulysses S. Grant she's good enough."

"Well, I wouldn't say we were that bad," Ty disagreed, "but it didn't matter in your mom's case. You two definitely share the 'hot chick' gene. Trust me on that one."

My face heated again. "I bow to your wisdom, sir. Back to the subject, the only other thing of note since you left was my marriage to jerk-off."

"I wish I could blame it on booze but I was just stupid. My friends tried to warn me about him and I didn't listen. The ink wasn't even dry on the marriage certificate when I caught him and Dora on the couch."

My jaw ached from the pressure I was putting into grinding my teeth so I forced myself to unclench. I took a deep breath before continuing. "I'm much better off without him dragging me down. They deserve one another. Good riddance."

He nodded slowly. "I think you're on the right track but it still stings, doesn't it? I could see the fire in your eyes this morning. It must be an iron-clad bitch to have them as your competition."

I shrugged. "Not really, as long as I don't have to see or speak to them."

"Have you ever considered getting even?"

"Revenge?" I shook my head. "No. That kind of stuff comes back to haunt you. I'm not ready for that kind of bad karma. I'll just let the world take care of it for me."

He slowly smiled, a wicked gleam in his eye. "No doubt the world will pick the right person for the job. You're absolutely right to take the high road. Leave the low road for those best suited for it."

I frowned. What was he getting at?

"But enough about you," he said with an unrepentant grin. "Let's talk about me."

"Okay, big guy," I agreed. "Where did you disappear to? The Navy, right?"

He nodded. "Yup. I joined up as a diver. Later on I was recruited for the SEAL teams. I did that for the last eight years."

I blinked. "A seal. Like in balancing a ball on your nose?" I clapped my hands together and made seal noises.

Ty snorted his coffee and started laughing. "That's not quite what I meant, but you get points for delivery. I'm talking about Navy Special Forces. Sea, Air, and Land."

"I've heard of Special Forces before," I admitted. "They talk about them on the news sometimes. Usually it's about the war in Afghanistan and Iraq."

He used his napkin to clean up the spewed coffee and nodded. "I went to both before I left the service. It wasn't fun."

"What?" I asked lightly. "No war stories? I thought veterans liked to impress the girls with their exploits and scars."

"There's nothing romantic about war," he said a touch grimly. "Particularly these more recent conflicts. You never know when some fanatic is going to pop up and fire an RPG at you. Or when the car next to you is going to blow up." He made an expansive gesture with his hands, like an explosion. "Then you have the more than occasional IED – Improvised Explosive Devices – planted by the road to kill the unwary.

When you go in after the jerks they just hide behind other people, bystanders get hurt or killed, and we catch the blame. The better we do militarily, the worse our image with the locals."

I blinked at his vehemence and I gently put a hand on his arm. "I'm sorry. I didn't mean to touch a nerve. Forget I mentioned it."

He took a deep breath and let it out slowly. "It's okay," he said. "I don't talk about it that often. When I do, my frustration leaks out. I'm sorry about that."

"Why don't we talk about something else," I said, changing the subject. "Like Steven Armstrong."

He nodded. "Damn poor luck on his part. More people die in the bathtub than falling off a dock."

"If he fell all by himself."

Ty's coffee cup paused on the way to his mouth. "You think he had help?" "I don't know. It just seems too coincidental. Stepping right on one spot of grease, falling just so." I shrugged. "It's possible but I can't help wondering if he made someone mad at him. If so, I'm worried the Sheriff's Department will go with the simplest explanation."

He shook his head. "If he was murdered, then they will figure it out. You're not thinking about playing Miss Marple, are you?"

I shrugged. "All I have are some questions. How dangerous can that be?"

He laughed. "Ask Armstrong. Asking questions might be nothing, if this was an accident. If it wasn't, you might just get the interest of someone that wouldn't be shy about venting his displeasure. Let it go, Candy. Let them do their job."

I wanted to argue, but our food arrived before I could get started. Karen balanced a big tray on one hand with grace that always amazed me. In her other hand was a folding stand that she adroitly popped open and set the tray neatly onto it. "One English muffin for the lady, and one of everything else for the gentleman."

His breakfast was big enough to keep me in food for a week. Karen laid it all out and refilled our coffee before sashaying away to handle the growing morning crowd.

When my muffin was gone, I stole a couple of pieces of bacon from his plate and ate them slowly with guilty delight.

"How long have you known Armstrong?" I asked.

"I met him a few months back when he hired me for hard-suit diving and salvage work. We've gotten together a few times since then for planning. I wouldn't say I really know him, though."

I nodded. "You're here in Angel's Point so the work must be about to start. When did you get here?"

"I checked into Fletcher Inn yesterday afternoon. He met with me before the dinner to finalize the operational plans. We also went over some technical details he wanted to have handy at the Lake Tahoe Mariner's Association dinner last night."

"I was at the one last year," I admitted. "They had it right here. As I recall, it was pretty stuffy."

"Not last night's dinner. It was a lot more exciting than I expected."

"Really?" I leaned forward eagerly. "What happened?"

"Word of his salvage plans leaked. Some of his associates were more than a little torqued about it. There was some resentment about raising an historic relic like the SS Tahoe. There was some grumbling and a few people were downright hostile." He shrugged. "I wouldn't call it a brawl, but harsh words and a couple of threats were exchanged.

A big fight at the Inn? That wouldn't reflect well on Calvin and Dora when it got around. I made a mental note to start some juicy rumors. "How harsh?"

He leaned back. "Well, let's see. One of the guests called him 'an arrogant ass' and called his plan a publicity stunt that the LTMA didn't need their president involved with. You know Armstrong was the Association president this year, right?"

I shook my head and let him continue.

"Well, he was. That one guy tried to get the group to vote against the project. Armstrong just sneered him down. Said he didn't need his 'precious permission.' I gather that there was more than a little bad blood between the two."

It would've been fun to be at that meeting. "What was the mood of the crowd? Were they with Armstrong or against him?"

Ty shrugged. "I gathered about two-thirds either supported him or didn't care. The other third grumbled, but only the one guy was hell bent to stop the deal, at least at first."

Do you know his name?"

One corner of his mouth quirked upward. "I couldn't have missed hearing it. His last name is Stanton. I doubt that his full name is 'that ass Stanton', though."

I laughed.

"That wasn't the last of it, either. Another man showed after we started eating. On a personal note, the food here is much better. The second guy was even more entertaining than Stanton. In a wild-eyed fanatical way. He kicked his way through the main door to the dining room and denounced Armstrong before your ex-husband and his wife dragged him off."

"Wow. It sounds like I missed one hell of a party."

"I think the man was with one of the Lake Tahoe preservation societies. I didn't catch the name, but that was the thrust of what he said. He said they'd never allow Armstrong to disturb the ship. He sounded righteously pissed."

I finished my coffee while I considered that.

"Will losing Armstrong kill the recovery effort?"

Ty shook his head. "I don't think so. Armstrong had a partner who's just as gung-ho about this project as he was. Damien Manchester."

He finished his breakfast and sighed regretfully. "Speaking of Mister Manchester, I should track him down. We've got a lot to talk about."

I looked down at the table, astonished that all the food in front of Ty was gone. Reluctant for breakfast to be over, and not sure why I was feeling that way, I took his hand in mine and looked up into his face. "Thanks for being here this morning. It's been good seeing you again."

He stood up and gave me a two finger salute. "I think we might be seeing each other more often than you think. See you around." With that and a sexy swagger of his hips he walked out the door.

Damn all good looking men!

THE END

ABOUT THE AUTHOR

Sir Patrick Bijou is an eclectic writer, lives in the United Kingdom and was born in 1958 in Georgetown and raised in London, England.

His diverse writing prowess has been influenced by my many experiences.

He pursued several courses of study at several universities and declared two majors during his schooling which included the areas of Business and Economics and finally obtained his doctorate in Economics and International banking.

In all these scholastic studies though, the true treasures I took away are not the certificates (though those are very important), but instead the experiences I had, the people I met, the foods I ate and even the places I stayed in.

In truth, I am a citizen of the world and this greatly influences my writing.

So, if you are already a fan of mine, I appreciate you. If you are not yet one, then what are you waiting for? Read a book and then read some more. I create characters that resonate with you and infuse life into all I write.

Finding my Books

I have written over 12 fictional and non-fictional books written across several genres and intending to do so for the rest of my writing career, I have realized the need to make it easier for my readers to find my books.

www.ingramcontent.com/pod-product-compliance
Lightning Source LLC
Chambersburg PA
CBHW070943120726
47908CB00005BA/1500